Can a Princess be a Firefighter?

By Carole P. Roman

Illustrated by Mateya Arkova

For Hallie and Cayla- "If you can dream it, you can do it."
Walt Disney

Special thanks to Bianca Schulze,
Julie Gerber, Conny Crisalli,
and Margie Takala

My band of sisters.

"Can a princess be a firefighter?"

you ask when I look down.

"Gowns that judges wear are neat,"
you say.

"And match my sparkly crown."

"You can be anything you want to be, anywhere, place, or time.

Dancer, dentist, cowpoke, reporter,

painter, biologist, accountant, or mime."

You think a bit, then tell me,

"I'd love to do all those things."

"Will I have to stop princessing?" you ask.

"Could I still wear my fairy wings?"

"Doctors are smart; inventors work hard, and truckers drive all day.

Construction workers have to be strong; sculptors work with clay.

You can be anything you want to be,
anywhere, place, or time.
Artist, explorer, lawyer, nurse,
mayor, pilot, or even fight crime.

19

You can run for office, work in a zoo, model clothes, or be in the navy.

Join the circus, deliver the mail,

or be a chef serving up tasty gravy.

Astronaut, farmer, teacher, mom,
just to name a few.
Hummm, with so many great opportunities,

did it ever occur that you could do two?

There are some things you need to know;
you can always change your mind.

Don't let anybody limit your dreams.

You are smart, talented, sweet, and kind.

Once you grow up, you'll go to work,"

I add along the way.

"It's important that you like your job.

It should make you happy every day.

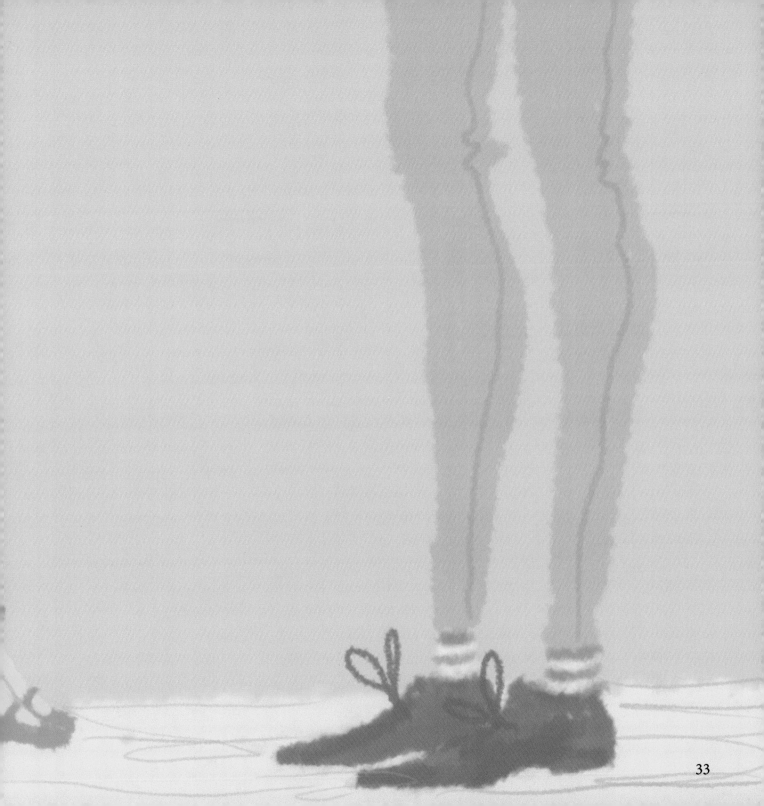

So, my dears, whatever you pick,
whatever you choose to be,
know that in my true heart,
you will always be
a princess to me."

CPSIA information can be obtained at www.ICGtesting.com
Printed in the USA
LVIW01n1511141116
512904LV00012B/104